As With Any Angel
A Lesson

Michael L. Piazza

Copyright © 2014 Michel L. Piazza

All rights reserved.

DEDICATION

Dedicated to my wife Linda and her friend Nevada...the inspirations for this story.

CONTENTS

Chapter 1   Page 1

Chapter 2   Page 10

Chapter 3   Page 18

Chapter 4   Page 22

Chapter 5   Page 32

CHAPTER 1

"Who is that," the gray haired Mrs. Harris said, peering thru the window into the parking lot.

Mrs. Harris along with several of the other ladies of the church congregation were putting the final touches on the Wednesday fellowship dinner. This Wednesday night's dinner featured chili and soup to counter the winter chill. Mrs. Harris and Mrs. Lake were at the sink in front of the large window to the parking lot washing some pots as others were preparing to serve their home cooked feast.

"Let me see, dear," Mrs. Lake said, pushing her face against the cold window glass next to Mrs. Harris. "Looks like some kind of vagrant or homeless person. Oh, dear, I hope he doesn't expect anything from us. The smell of such a person will just ruin our supper."

"Maybe he'll just go away," Mrs. Harris said with an exasperated tone.

"What ya'll gawking at?" chided David Tackett walking up behind the two older ladies. "See a ghost or something?"

"Worse!" Mrs. Harris said pointing at the figure standing the parking lot. "A bum! Or something! I'm sure that he is going to come in here with his hand out expecting us to give him supper or something. Why can't those people just stay in their own part of town and go to the shelters. I mean, this church contributes a lot of money to those shelters! Why must they come here for more? What is this world coming to?"

"Yes, mam," David said, peering thru the glass, "he looks unkept to me. I'll take care of this, you ladies just keep on with your fixin's. I know how to tend to his kind."

David headed towards the double glass doors of the large fellowship hall. He is a tall man, early sixties, but in great shape. He played college football at a popular state university and is known throughout the state for his still standing records as a wide receiver. All of the ladies in the church love him. He is a widower of three years and is always charming and protective. It is a natural event in their small congregation for 'Mr. Tackett to take charge' in a situation such as this.

"Trouble, David?" Pastor Tom Reynolds said to David as he passed by the table where the Pastor and his wife were seated, waiting for the fellowship supper to begin.

"Nothing big, Reverend," David said as he passed by the seated Pastor, "just someone at the wrong place. Be back in a jiff."

"Let me know if I can be of assistance," the Pastor said, sipping his coffee.

"Will do," David said opening the large glass door.

The night had brought a dramatic lowering of the temperature. The Mississippi winter weather is fairly predictable. High into the lower fifty degree mark during the afternoon, then dropping into the forties by early evening, then into thirties by morning. The temperature at eight p.m. was in the lower forties. A steady light drizzling rain had been falling since early morning. The kind of weather that 'makes the bones ache and the body shake.'

"Can I help ya', buddy?" David said in an assertive tone as he approached the figure in the parking lot.

"I, ah," stammered the trembling man, "don't know how to ask for help. I, ah, just don't know where else to go."

"There are shelters in the town about three miles that way," David said pointing east on the highway. "Why don't you go there? I'm sure they can help you."

"I, ah, can pay," the man said quivering as he pulled a small bundle of money from his pocket. "I am so cold and my feet hurt...I am not sure where I am. I will be glad to pay for a bowl of soup or a cup of coffee."

David stood rigid for a moment analyzing the man. His first thought was that the man had stolen the money from somewhere. It was too much for a vagrant to have. The light from the street light was bright enough for him to determine that the man was in his late thirties or early forties. He was wearing clothes that at one time were fairly expensive, but were now worn and faded. The man had on what seemed to be expensive Italian dress shoes that had very little sole left on either shoe. The right shoe had a small hole over the big toe. David presumed them to be throw outs from the closet an affluent person which had been donated to a homeless shelter. He had taken many of his own worn out suits, shirts and shoes to such places. He had never actually seen someone wearing the once expensive throw-aways. David thought it was somehow ironic, but at the same time a contradiction. Worn out expensive clothes on a bum. A faded suit for a fading life.

"I will be glad to pay whatever is a fair price," the man said, his voice cracking and his body trembling, "I just don't think I can go any farther without something to eat..."

"Look, buddy," David said patronizingly, "there's no way that we can take your money. The thing is, there are some real decent folks in there. This is a special night for them, especially the old folks. They don't get out much. I don't mean to be blunt, but it might be best if you just move along. This is a private affair for good church people. A special night, you know what I mean?"

"I can pay..." the man said, shaking from the cold.

"It's not the money," David said in a stronger tone, wishing the man would take the hint and leave. "It's simply that this is a special night for these people. Don't you understand that? Now, it'll be best for all of us if you just go on down the road. These are decent people in there; do you know what I am saying to you?"

"Yes, ah, yes I do," the man said softly, "I have said those same words to someone like me before. Please, sir, I don't need to come in, I will gladly stay out here. I am just so hungry..."

"Hey, Mr. David," a young voice said from behind David, "Mrs. Harris said that everything is ready and the Pastor is about to bless the food."

David looked around and saw Mitsy, the twelve year old granddaughter of Mrs. Lake. He didn't want the child to see the quivering mass of a human standing in front of him. David liked to protect people from such things.

"Thanks, little lady," David said stepping between Mitsy and the smelly, tattered man. "Go on back inside and I'll be right behind you," he said to her, trying his best to block her view of the stranger two feet from him.

"Are you all right, mister?" Mitsy said, leaning around David. "You don't look so good! You had better come inside and get warm."

"He's alright, Mitsy!" David interrupted. "The gentleman was just on his way. Now, do like I told you and go on inside. I'll be right behind you."

"But, Mr. David," Mitsy said stepping around the large man, "this man is shaking and doesn't even have a rain coat on. He needs to come inside and get warm. My name is Mitsy," the young girl said, extending her tender hand around David and toward the trembling figure.

"Don't!" David said loudly, stopping the young girl's hand from touching the stranger's hand. "You don't know if he is sick, or where he has been or anything, child! Don't touch him; he might have some kind of disease!"

David pulled Mitsy by her hand and quickly returned to the building. He raced over to the girl's grandmother and told her what had happened outside and warned her about Mitsy's ignorance. Mrs. Lake kindly, but sternly corrected Mitsy for her error. Mitsy tried to object, but the people started lining up in the pot luck supper line. "Not now, child," Mrs. Lake said, "but we'll discuss this later."

As the small crowd enveloped the two, Mitsy eased away from her grandmother and walked to the window. The man was still standing in the parking lot. She decided that when everyone was eating dessert and the members of the youth group were cleaning the dishes, she would take a plate of food out to the stranger. "As you do for the least of these, you do for me," she said to herself. She had heard those words said many times around the church. She became determined that she would do a good thing for this stranger that had come to their pot luck supper needing a meal. There was always plenty left over. She knew that no one would miss whatever she took to him.

Just as the last dinner plate was put in the kitchen area and all of the adults were starting to choose their desserts, Mitsy piled some of the leftovers onto a paper plate. She grabbed a plastic fork and knife, a couple of paper napkins and then disappeared thru the hallway. For the next several minutes she was not missed.

The youth group had already begun their chores when Mrs. Harris and Mrs. Lake came into the kitchen to brew some more coffee. They looked around and did not see Mitsy.

"She loaded up a plate and took off down the hallway," one of the young boys spoke up, "said something about doing for the least of me, or something like that."

"David!" Mrs. Lake said loudly. "David!" she said almost running into the fellowship hall. "I think Mitsy has gone outside to that bum again!" She was frantic. "Please help me!" she cried.

David jumped up and ran to the window. He strained his eyes looking into the rainy parking lot. Then terror struck him. The man was lying on the ground and it looked like he had pulled Mitsy down next to him. His heart raged as his mind raced. David pictured the horrible possibilities of what may be happening. "Stay here," he said to Mrs. Lake and then he broke into a long stride, similar to his football days. The Pastor and a couple of the other men saw him running and immediately pushed away from their tables and followed behind him.

As David entered the parking lot he could hear Mitsy weeping. A hundred thoughts ran thru David's head as he strained his eyes to see what the vagrant was doing to this precious child. Questions pierced his being. Why had she not heeded his warning? Why had she disobeyed her grandmother? Thoughts of fear, rage and intolerance raced one after another thru his mind with each pounding step of his gallop.

"Let go of her!" David screamed as he neared the scene. "You hurt that child and I will rip your heart out," David said intensely.

He stopped just over the girl, gasping to catch his breath. His heart pounded. He strained his eyes in the dimly lit parking lot trying to determine just where and how the man was molesting this young and innocent child. He fell to his knees, angrily looking for the man's arms to grab them away from the girl. He looked twice and could not make out any physical contact, yet Mitsy was weeping deeply.

"Run, child!" David said out of breath, "I'll take care of this bum!"

Mitsy didn't move. She was on her knees, very near to the man's head. She was holding the plate of food in her hands. She stared at the man and continued to weep. Pastor Reynolds and the other men now crowded around the three member scene.

As With Any Angel

The stranger was laid out straight with his face down on the asphalt. Mitsy, kneeling only inches from his head, the plate of food drenched from the light rain. David was still frantically looking over the man to find some place of physical contact, ready to strike the man at any moment. There was an intense moment of confusion. No one was really sure what was happening.

"He, he," Mitsy stammered, involuntarily repeating her words with the intense rhythm of the breathing from her sobbing, "wo…, would, not answer me!" she cried. "He, he, is gone!" she sobbed.

Pastor Reynolds knelt down beside her and stared at the man on the ground. The man's eyes were open, but they were not moving. The Pastor gently placed his hand on the man's neck. The man did not flinch or in any way respond. After a moment, the Pastor looked at David and shook his head. "No pulse," he said lowly.

"What?" David said, still excited, "what do you mean?"

"Mitsy's right," Pastor said, "he's gone."

"That can't be," David said, adrenalin still pumping thru his body, "he was…it looked like…he had to have done something…I mean the girl looked like…"

"That's alright, David," Pastor Reynolds said, "you did right, but it's all over now. Come child, let's get you inside before you get sick. Come everyone," the Pastor said to the people standing in the drizzling rain, "let's go back inside. There's nothing we can do but cover him until the paramedics get here. Let's go."

The Pastor tried to pry the plate out of Mitsy's hand but she wouldn't let go. "I need, need, to give this to him," she sobbed, "he was so hun, hungry and cold."

"You tried child," Pastor Reynolds said softly, "come on inside, there's nothing more you can do."

"Nooooooo!" she shouted, "we must do for him, we must help him. As for the least of these, please!" She was near hysteria.

Pastor Reynolds managed to get the plate out of her hand and then he picked her up from the cold, wet concrete and carried her inside. He took her into his office and gently set her down onto the large couch opposite of his desk. Mrs. Lake and Mrs. Harris quickly entered the Pastor's office and began to care for the sobbing young girl. David stood in the hallway just outside the doorway to the Pastor's office.

The paramedics were quick to respond and were there within minutes. They loaded the body of the stranger into the ambulance and then one of them came inside and checked Mitsy. She was still crying but not as uncontrollably as before. The paramedic, a young woman in her late twenties, calmly checked all of Mitsy's vital signs. She lighted nodded to the two ladies and then to the Pastor and David that the young girl was okay.

"Can't you give her something?" Mrs. Lake said frantically, "I am her grandmother and can sign any release forms. She needs something to calm her down. Please. Give her something."

"With what she has seen tonight," the young woman said, removing the stethoscope from around her neck, "she needs something that doesn't come from a pill or a needle."

"And what is that, young lady?" Mrs. Lake asked confused and a bit defensive.

"An answer," Pastor Reynolds said softly.

"That," the paramedic said placing her stethoscope in her small medical bag, "and something to believe in and hold onto."

"Well," Mrs. Lake said, flustered, "I understand all of those nice and philosophical thoughts, but at this moment I believe that what medical science can give her is what will bring immediate relief. If this lady won't give her something," Mrs. Lake said to Pastor Reynolds, "do you think that we should call Dr. Rankin?"

As the two ladies and the Pastor discussed what they

should do, the young paramedic leaned close to Mitsy and spoke very softly into her ear. As the young woman quietly spoke into her ear, Mitsy started to catch her breath and ceased her crying. The young woman continued to speak softly to the exhausted young child on the couch.

Mitsy rubbed her eyes and looked deep into the eyes of the young woman paramedic. "Are you sure?" Mitsy asked in a very childish tone.

"Yep, sure as I can be," the young woman answered. She gently stroked Mitsy's hair and lightly rubbed her temples. Mitsy closed her eyes and after a few moments appeared to go to sleep.

"We're ready to go, Lieutenant," came a male voice from the doorway of the Pastor's office.

"Okay, be right there," the woman said standing. "If she wakes up and can't get back to sleep," she said handing a small plastic package to Mrs. Lake, "give her one these. It will help her sleep thru the night."

Everyone, except for Mitsy and the two ladies in the Pastor's office, was on the sidewalk when the ambulance pulled away. There was a subdued murmur as the crowd dispersed, some to their cars, others back into the fellowship hall to retrieve their empty dishes before leaving. Most everyone said a word of thanks or congratulation to David Tackett on their way out. Everyone was glad that he was there to handle such a nasty situation.

CHAPTER 2

The remainder of the week was a trying time for the small congregation. As word spread of the stranger that stalked their Wednesday night pot luck supper, rumor added to rumor. The small city was buzzing with overblown stories of Wednesday night. Many in the congregation were astonished at what was being said about the seemingly simple chain of events.

Some had heard a rumor that said that the man had raped poor Mitsy and that David Tackett, the old football hero, had to throw himself against the raging man to get him off of her. His blow knocked the man hard to the asphalt and the impact had caused the man's head to strike the ground with enough force to kill him. Others had heard a rumor which said that the stranger had knocked David down and that someone else in the congregation had to shoot the assailant.

Regardless of the facts, the small church was the buzz of the city's news. An exciting rape and heroic saving by a football hero that ended in the death of the stranger. Eventually, the Pastor had to ask each of the local television stations to run a factual story of the actual events of the night so that these rumors could cease. Even though all of the stations cooperated, some people still refused to believe the boring story of a homeless man dying at the feet of a young girl trying to give him a meal. They preferred to keep alive an exciting story of rape, heroic defense and mysterious death.

Being true to their southern traditions, and also being very polite Southerners, no one mentioned the Wednesday night event before, during, or after Sunday services. They all gave that Southern facial expression that indicated "we're gonna be alright, no use in any of us talking about it." The subject was intentionally left without words. Much to many's surprise, Mitsy was not at the service. Her mother had taken her to the gulf coast to visit relatives for the weekend. She believed the change would do Mitsy a world of good and help her recover from the trauma of the event.

David was the unsung hero of the day. Though everyone knew that the trumped up stories of heroism were not true, they still gave David the respect and honor that would go to such a hero. It was as though the people, especially the members of the congregation, needed to believe that some of the rumors were true. Even if they weren't. Even if they had witnessed the actual events for themselves and knew them to be untrue. But still, there was a need to pretend, a need to feel secure and pay false respects to their hero.

To have a homeless man die just outside of a fellowship hall that was full of food and heat was not something that anyone liked to think about. On the other hand, thwarting the attempt of a viscous vagrant trying to rape a twelve year old was much more honorable. At least, it was much easier to rationalize and accept.

Pastor Reynolds had tried to diffuse the confusion that morning with a sermon on Lazarus, focusing on how Jesus was just a short distance from his good friend when he died. He implored the congregation to seek a meaning in the incident, to explore the feelings that Martha and Mary may have experienced. He was not sure if it had any impact. He wasn't sure what he should do next. It was a confusing Sunday.

On the following Tuesday morning, the Pastor was on the telephone when he looked out his office window and saw David's car pulling up. It was a common site to see David stop by the church. He is generous with both his time and his money, especially since the death of his wife three years before. Pastor Reynolds knew he should locate David while he was at the church that morning and try to broach the subject of the past week's events with him. Southern etiquette or not, David would sooner or later need to openly and frankly discuss the situation in order to put it behind him. Before Pastor Reynolds could get off of the phone, David was standing at his door.

"Hello, David," Pastor said, hanging up the phone.

"Richard Dunning," David said, red-faced and very nervous, "Tom, the man was Richard Dunning."

"Who?" Pastor asked confused.

"Richard Dunning!" David said emphatically, "you know, Dunning Enterprises."

"Yes," Pastor Reynolds replied, "I remember Dunning Enterprises. But who is Richard Dunning?"

"The man in the parking lot!" David said exasperated, pacing in front of the desk. "It all makes sense now. The clothes, the shoes, the money. If I would have just known, I would have done something!"

"Settle down, David," Pastor Reynolds said, "tell me what you are talking about."

"I had my buddy at the Highway Patrol release to me the ID information on the guy that died in our parking lot the other night," David said, leaning over the desk on a few inches from the Pastor's face. "The guy was Richard Dunning. You see, Tom," David said flopping exhausted into the chair behind him, "I noticed the expensive clothes and shoes. They were worn out, but I could still tell they were high dollar. If I would have known it was one of the Dunning's, Jesus Christ, I would have done something! Anything!"

There was a silence between the two men. David stared out the window. Pastor Reynolds watched David's pain consume him. He knew that it was not a good time to lecture David on any element of the event. David was obviously too upset to rationally discuss anything related to it. But he couldn't just let the comment concerning the Dunning family pass without some comment.

"So, David," Tom said, "would it have really made a difference? Or are you just looking for an answer? When we've had some time for this to pass, we'll look at the..."

"You bet you sweet ass it would have made a difference," David said loudly. "I mean, I thought this guy was some no count bum! A waste of space. But for Christ's sake he was a Dunning! I know their fortune crashed with the stock market thing, but my God they are still an honorable family and one of good stead in the community. I would have taken him to the hospital, called somebody from that family, or something! If I would have just known!"

"But, David," Tom said, trying to calm his friend, "at that moment, he was who he was. There is no way that you could tell anything more than what you saw. Obviously the loss of their fortune took away the man's will to live, or who knows what circumstances led up to the other night. But, you can't hold yourself to blame for his misfortune. You just said he had money on him, he could have done differently if he chose to."

"He tried to buy..." David mumbled his words.

"He tried to what?" Tom asked kindly. "I couldn't hear what you were saying."

Tears began to roll down David's face. "He tried to buy a damn bowl of soup!" David said, his voice cracking.

"I don't understand," Tom said sincerely.

"For Christ's sake," David said intensely, "he tried to pay me for a bowl of soup and I told him that decent people were inside and to move along to his own kind!" David stared out the window and lightly wept.

"Oh, David," Tom said walking around the desk, "let your Spirit up off of the ground."

"No!" David yelled. "What kind of person won't sell a meal to a man who is dying from starvation? I killed the poor guy," David wept, "don't you understand what I am trying to tell you!"

"Oh, David, David, David," the Pastor said, placing his hand on his friend's shoulder. "Your contact at the Highway Patrol only told you the man's identification. He should have told you the whole story. The man in our parking lot, regardless of where he came from socially or what happened to his life; he died of some very severe illnesses. He did not die from hunger."

"What are you talking about?" David said trying to regain control of his emotions.

"You've got to let this go," Tom said compassionately. "The man had advanced liver damage and severe heart blockage. He died of a combination of the two. The official death certificate says he died from a heart attack." Tom leaned forward and looked into David's eyes. "He would have died that night anyway. Food or no food, or whatever. He was a very sick man on his last leg."

"It still doesn't change what I did, though," David said sadly.

"I don't believe that the Lord holds you in anyway responsible for..."

"No," David said weakly, "don't you see. I have spent my entire life trying to impress people. I am an old man and what am I doing? I'm still trying to impress a couple of old women. I had no intention of doing anything when I walked out the door Wednesday night but playing big shot. I wanted to be the big man that ran that bum out of our parking lot. Then, I noticed his clothes. He spoke to me.

But I couldn't look at his face, his eyes, or anything. I just wanted him to go away so that I could look good in the eyes of those women. In your eyes. In the congregation's eyes. David Tackett, the hero and star who saved the congregation's social night by braving the cold and rain to chase a bum away! And then he dies. I ran away from him."

"Don't bury yourself with him," Pastor said, "he had already chosen his path. You can still..."

"I grabbed that little girl and told her to get away from him," David said standing and pacing again. "But she had the courage to go back out there and take him some food. Courage that I didn't have. She did what we are supposed to do! But no, my fear, my ego! I had to run away and make everyone think I had done some deed of valor when a twelve year old girl was the only one brave enough to do the right thing!"

"But, David," Tom said, standing in front of David to stop him from pacing, "Mitsy doesn't believe you are to blame for this man. She was told about his condition. She understands that he would have died one way or another. She also understands that she was wrong in disobeying what she had been told to do. What if those horrible thoughts that ran thru our hearts when we saw her in the dark with him had actually happened? What if Mitsy had actually been assaulted as we all feared coming into the parking lot? Would you still think that she was so brave? You addressed the man, you asked him to leave, then you wisely brought Mitsy back inside. What is wrong with all of that? You did what anyone would have done in your..."

"You are such a nice guy," David said cynically, "but you still don't get it. All of that was a show. I was scared stiff of that man. The sight of him petrified me. But my ego made me go out and try to run him away. But that little girl had courage...courage enough to sneak food out to him. I don't even have the guts of a twelve year old girl. Do you get what I am saying? Is it sinking in?"

"Then talk to her," Tom said quickly. "Listen to what she has to say about that night. Let her know that you were sincerely trying to protect her. Let her tell you that she doesn't hold you responsible. She believes that you were right when you told her not to touch the man. She knows that you were correct when you told her that he may be very sick and possibly contagious. She thinks that you were meant to be there to protect her and keep her safe from evil..."

"That's all such crap!" David yelled. "I was scared! I hated that this man came to our parking lot. Rushing her back inside was my excuse to run away from him. Usually people like that just go away. But he didn't! Now look at this mess. I was glad that child was not at church Sunday. I would not have been able to face her. How can I tell her I was no hero? Everybody in this town believes I saved this child from harm! The truth is that I ran away like a scared kid. And she, she was the one with the courage to march outside and try to help him."

"She's coming here tomorrow at ten," Tom said assertively. "Come here then and meet with her. The two of you can help each other get past this thing. She has a lot of unresolved issues in her life that have become really tied up because of this thing. Somehow, I know in my heart that the two of you need to face yourselves and at the same time face each other. Try to be here while she's here. Honest feelings shared from both of you might bring a miraculous end to this nightmare."

"Yeah, right!" David said sarcastically and then stormed out of the Pastor's office. He slammed the door to the church as he left the building. Pastor Reynolds stood at his window and watched David wheel his car backwards from the parking space and then accelerate out thru the parking lot.

Pastor Reynolds sat back in his chair and sighed deeply, lightly shaking his head. He remembered how excited he was on the way to the pot luck supper last Wednesday night. In his meditation earlier that Wednesday morning, it had been revealed to him that something special would happen at the gathering that night, and that it would be a very special life changing event.

"Well, Lord," Tom said to the empty room, "I sure wish you would share with me the dictionary that you used when you called that night 'special.' It was special alright," he said rubbing his temples, "and life changing. No one in this small congregation has been the same since."

CHAPTER 3

The next morning David stopped by the church as usual. When he rounded the corner in the hallway just down from the Pastor's office he glanced at his watch. It was thirty minutes past ten. He slowed his pace as he heard the voice of a young person. He walked very softly on the carpet so as not to be heard. He thought the young girl would be gone by this time, but fear gripped him as he realized that she may still be in the Pastor's office.

As he entered the outer office of the Pastor's area, he could hear Mitsy talking to Pastor Reynolds. He froze. He didn't know what to do. He wanted to turn and walk away. But at the same time he wanted to join them. He stood still and pretended to be reading something on the vacant receptionist's desk, just in case there was someone else in the building. He didn't want it to be obvious that he was eaves dropping on the Pastor and the young girl.

"No, sir," Mitsy said in her cute little southern accent, "I didn't see him. Sissy told me about what he said."

"Sissy?" Pastor inquired.

"Yes, sir," she continued, "the paramedic lady."

"Oh, you mean the Lieutenant," he responded. "Is her name Sissy?"

"Yes, sir, I read it on her shirt. Sissy Williams," Mitsy said in a childish tone, "I'll never forget it."

"Oh, I guess I was too busy with all that was going on to notice her name tag," Pastor Reynolds said. "She was very nice and very calm."

"She sent me a card the other day," Mitsy chuckled. "It said, 'you're okay, and pretty brave, even if you are just a twelve year old kid." They both laughed. David smiled to himself.

"So," Pastor Reynolds queried, "tell me more about what Sissy told you this angel said to her?"

David panicked at those words. He had heard that Mitsy had claimed to see angels since the tragic death of her father. David was afraid that last week's trauma may have seriously compounded the confused emotions of young Mitsy. He wanted to leave before he heard anymore. But for some reason, he couldn't move his feet. It was as though he was frozen to the floor.

"Sissy said that the man's angel was there when they got there," Mitsy said shyly. "She said that the angel had told her that he had just taken the man to heaven. And then the angel told Sissy to tell me thank you for trying to give that man some food, but that it was already time for them to leave for heaven when I walked outside. The angel said he couldn't wait for the man to eat, that he had to take him to heaven right then. When the angel got back from taking the man to heaven and tried to tell me thanks for bringing him some food, I was inside and the ambulance people were there instead. So the angel told Sissy to tell me thanks."

"And she told you this that night when you were laying there on the couch?"

"Yes, sir," Mitsy said proudly, "and she said my angel was there, too. Ever since my Daddy was killed, I have had angels watching over me."

"And you believe one of them was there with you that night?" Pastor asked carefully.

"Yes, sir," she said smiling, "there is always one close by me. Sometimes, when I get real scared, I concentrate real hard and then I feel one close to me. You know," Mitsy said wrinkling her brow, "I think Mr. David was my angel that night. He watched over me and made sure I was safe. He is such a strong man, and b-i-g!" she said, reaching her hands over her head pantomiming his height.

David was ashamed when he heard young Mitsy call him an angel. He began to shake. He was afraid he was going to lose control. David took off running for the bathroom. He flung the door open and then immediately started banging his fists against the cinder block walls. He was disgusted with himself. He turned and looked at his reflection in the mirror.

"You fake!" he said to his own strained eyes, tears streaming down his red cheeks. "This little girl thinks you are some kind of protective angel and you are nothing but a washed up old coward who didn't even have the courage to sell a bowl of soup to a poor, dying man! Then you ran away like a freekin' coward, but that child mustered more courage than you have in your being..."

"Are you talking to me?" came a startled voice from around the small partition by the first stall.

David jumped at the sound of the voice. He quickly grabbed a paper towel and wiped his face.

"Were you talking to me, sir?" asked the voice again.

"Ah, no, I, ah," David stammered. He turned and saw a young man he had not seen before standing at the sink next to him. "I, ah, just...am letting a little steam off."

"Well, sir," the young man said respectfully, "with the events of the last week, I believe that you definitely have a lot of steam to let off."

"Excuse me?" David said defensively.

"Yeah," the young man said washing his hands, looking at David in the mirror, "using that little girl as an excuse to run away from one of the unpleasant social ills of our society. Pretty lame if you ask me. Now, she thinks that you were some kind of angel there to watch over her for that night. Yes, sir, I guess that paradox would cause anyone to heat up and build up a bit of steam. Yes, sir, it sure would."

"Who the hell do you think you are, talking to me like that?" David demanded.

"That doesn't matter. What matters is, are you correct about yourself? Or is that little girl correct about you? Are you this ego driven coward, as you just accused yourself of?" the young man said very intensely. "Or, are you more afraid that the young girl is right? That your actions that night were somehow those of a guardian? I think that scares you more than believing that you were a coward. I think this coward stuff is a cop out! After all, you did stop her from touching the man; you did take her to her grandmother to see that she was corrected. Then, you did run with all of your might to save her when you thought that she was being attacked. I would think that only an angel could have been more intuitive and done a better job. So, she has you confused with her angel. Maybe she's right. Maybe you are what she says that you are and you just don't know it. Or, maybe you are simply afraid to admit it."

The man wiped his hands on a paper towel and tossed it into the trash can. He combed his short brown hair and did not look at David again. But David glared at the man, shocked at his brash and profoundly true statements that no one could possibly know. David was flabbergasted to the point that he was unable to speak, a new situation for him. David is never speechless.

The man casually walked to the door, stopped and turned to David. "But, of course, only three people know what really happened that night," the man said smiling. "Two of you are still alive to talk about it. Perhaps that will be your answer. The two of you talking about it." The man quickly left and the door slowly closed behind him..

CHAPTER 4

David vigorously splashed water on his face trying to get a grip on himself. His hands were shaking, his head was aching and his heart was pumping. He felt like he was on the verge of a breakdown of some kind. For a brief moment, staring into the bathroom mirror, he was hoping that this was all just a dream and that he would awaken from it. The door opened again and Tom Reynolds walked in. David knew that he was not in a dream.

"Oh, David," the Pastor said surprised, "I am so glad that you decided to come here today. Mitsy would really like to talk with...you," the Pastor stammered as he noticed the water all over David's face and on the fringes of his hairline. "Everything okay, David?" Pastor asked cautiously.

"Who was that guy that was just in here?" David said very perturbed.

"Do what?" Pastor replied.

"That young whippersnapper that was just in here," David said sternly. "If he comes back in here I'll kick his smart aleck little ass!"

"Settle down, David, if someone was rude to you in here we can deal with that later, but right now we need to help this child get a good step past a rough situation." The Pastor pulled several towels from the dispenser and handed them to David. "She really needs you right now. I don't know if it is just that the two of you are possibly sharing some kind of common survivors' syndrome or just what. But I really feel that you are somehow, and for some reason, spiritually tied together. It may all make sense soon. But for now, please, David, help me with this," he said handing more towels to David.

David finished wiping the water from his face, then left the bathroom and walked down the hallway towards the Pastor's office. David's stomach began to churn with a thousand butterflies. He has been so lonely since his wife had passed away. His two children are in their forties and live in the Northeast. He sees his grandchildren only on holidays and special occasions. He has seen them so infrequently that he feels like a grandfather in title only. It has been a very long time since he has had any kind of one-on-one interaction with a child, especially a troubled child.

As David neared the Pastor's office, he became increasingly unsure of himself. He knew that he didn't have it in him to try to deal the problems that were plaguing young Mitsy. He couldn't even cope with his own demons; much less help the Pastor chase hers away. He stopped in the outer office. He couldn't go into the Pastor's office. David felt that he was just not capable of trying to help Mitsy while he himself was so broken with the horrible inner feelings that had been consuming him for the past two days. He felt of no use to anyone. He decided that he would just leave before she saw him.

Before he could turn to leave, David felt the touch of a small hand on his left hand. He looked down at his hand and then saw Mitsy standing beside him. She had just come back into the office area from the kitchen. She squeezed David's hand and he impulsively lightly squeezed hers back.

"I am so sorry that I disobeyed you the other night," Mitsy said, looking at the floor, "you and Grandmamma were right. It was not safe for me to go outside by myself to that man. He was very sick and, well, anyway, I am sorry."

David eased down to his knees. With his height, on his knees he was a just a little below eye level of the petite stature of Mitsy. He held both of her hands and looked into her eyes. "I have a confession to make to you," he said, "the other night, I was scared..."

"Are you really going to wimp out like this?" interrupted a voice from behind Mitsy.

David looked up and saw the young man that had harassed him in the bathroom. "This child is in desperate need of hope, faith, courage, strength, and God knows what else," the young man said in a strong tone. "The fact is she sees all of those things in you. All of the faith and courage she needs is right there in front of her. And all you can do is moan and whine about how scared you were!"

The young man leaned over Mitsy and got right in David's face. "Well, maybe you sensed what was going on!" he chided. "Think about that. Maybe you knew the danger that the two of you were in and you snatched this child away from it. Maybe, she needed the courage and strength that surrounded her when you rushed to her side when you thought that she was being abused. Or maybe," the man said intensely, "maybe, she just loves you. She desperately needs to love someone. But you know what?" the man said arrogantly. "Your self-pity has blinded you. I heard what you said to the Pastor after I left the bathroom! If you really think you are man enough to kick my ass, just come on and give it a try. Right now, right here!" the young man said, egging David on. "Or," he said maliciously, his hand open and only inches from Mitsy's hair, "should I fight this little girl instead? Pull her precious hair from her head?" he taunted, his hand only an inch from Mitsy's forehead.

"You hurt this child and I will rip your heart out!" David hollered. He became very intense, like a rattle snake coiled to strike.

"That's exactly what you said to that man last Wednesday night," the young man said with a smile, backing back a step. "Hmm," the man said amused, "is there a pattern forming here?"

"How do you know what I said last Wednesday night?" David said angrily, still coiled and ready to strike.

The man smiled again and pointed to his feet. He pulled his pant leg up over his ankle. "Remember these?" he said. "See, there were three people there, remember?"

"Oh, my God!" David said in amazement. The man had on the same brand and color shoes that Richard Dunning was wearing that night. The same suit. Only new and fresh, not worn or soiled.

"Yes, oh your God, indeed," the young man chided, "now are you going to wimp out? Or are you going to give of yourself freely and faithfully to this lovely child? You have what she needs," the young man said passionately. "Why are you so afraid to share it with her? Please tell me that you are willing to help her. Let her think you are an angel if she needs to. She is waiting for you to help her? Gonna help or not?"

David looked back at Mitsy. Her sad young eyes looked frantically into his eyes, searching for some relief. His heart melted into the pit of his stomach. He looked back at the young man and nodded. "Yes, I'll help her."

"So, are you sure that is your answer?" the young man asked. "Can I take that to be a firm yes?"

David shook his head affirmatively. "Yes, I am certain…if I can."

He was very angry and confused at the young man but at the same time felt a sense of guidance from him. The young man was so much like David was when he was in his early years. Feisty, forceful, and wise. David's heart was burning with emotion.

"Then you must forget your fears from this point on. Otherwise, you will never help this young child to overcome hers," the young man said. "Do you understand that? Your fears, your regrets, they must cease. But the only way that they will cease is if you help Mitsy with her troubles. Can you understand? She will be for you, just what you will be for her. You both need each other. Is this making sense to you yet?"

David shook his head affirmatively.

"Who are you talking to, Mr. David?" Mitsy asked, tugging at David's hands. "Is there someone in the hallway?" she said with her small voice shaking. She looked over her shoulder and couldn't see anyone. She was becoming very afraid.

"Hunh?" David replied, looking at Mitsy's fearful expression. When he looked up again, the man was gone.

David felt like he had left the room and then suddenly returned. He looked again at Mitsy. He could tell that Mitsy had not seen the young man who had taunted him. David became weak. He felt like he was going to pass out. Reality was escaping him. He felt like he may be having a stroke, or maybe even a heart attack. David began to sag, barley holding himself up with his palms outstretched on the floor.

"Please, Mr. David, don't be sick!" Mitsy cried, starting to shake.

"Oh, I'm alright," David said, pulling together every ounce of strength left in him. He stood tall on his knees. "I'm sorry, what were we talking about?" he said softly to Mitsy.

"You were just starting to say that the other night...that you were scared…" Mitsy said looking at the floor, then back into David's eyes. "What are you scared of Mr. David? I didn't think you were scared of anything!" Her eyes were full of tears.

"Well, I wasn't really scared, not like that, it was just that, ah," David stammered for a moment, beginning to understand the deep and intense need in this child's eyes. "I was scared in another way. I...ah, thought that poor man was going to do something, like, ah, throw up or something. I don't know," David said trying to regain his composure. "It just didn't seem safe for you, or for me, to be out there with him. I know I probably should have helped him," he said taking a deep breath, "but I was scared in a good way...scared for you, and for me. I couldn't think of him at that moment. I could only think of you, and of me."

"I was scared at first, too," Mitsy said, "when I went back outside. I brought the man some food, then all of a sudden he just fell down. I kneeled down to help him, but he couldn't get back up. I didn't know what to do. I knew right then that I should not have gone back out there. I was so scared that I just couldn't move. I was so glad to hear you coming. I knew everything would be alright when I heard you coming. You made me feel safe again."

Mitsy leaned against David and placed her head on his shoulder. She began to cry. David lightly patted her back. David looked up and saw that the young man was standing behind Mitsy again. David started to speak but the young man quickly motioned for David not to speak. The young man turned and walked around behind David.

Suddenly, as the young man walked behind him, David felt the strength of his years beginning to return. While the child's tears rolled onto to his shoulder and pooled on his shirt, he felt a strength filling his being. The knots in his stomach that had been there for the last few years had started to disappear. In only a few short moments, at the depth of his weakness, and at the depth of Mitsy's weakness, the strength of his Spirit returned to him. He wasn't sure where the power was coming from, but he had not felt this level of inner strength in years. The words 'In your weakness you will know My strength' echoed in David's soul.

Pastor Reynolds entered the office and stopped, taking

in the site of the two. He looked at David's face. He could see a renewed peace in David's soul. The Pastor walked next to Mitsy and placed his hand on her head and lightly patted her hair. He could feel that her great fear had subsided. After a few moments of silence, Mitsy stopped crying and stood straight up again.

"Your grandmother is here," Pastor Reynolds told her. "Do you feel better now?" he asked. "Do you feel like going home?"

"Yes, sir," she smiled wiping the few straggling tears, "I feel much better now."

"Do you feel safe again?" Pastor asked her compassionately, nervously awaiting her answer.

"Yes, sir," she said without hesitation, resting her hand on David's chest, "I feel very safe, now. As safe as I would with any angel."

"Then let's go to the car," Pastor said reaching for her hand. "Your grandmother has been very worried about you. She will be glad to see you smiling again."

"Will you be here tonight?" Mitsy asked David, her hand still on his chest.

"It is Wednesday again, isn't it?" David chuckled. "You bet ya'," he said with a smile, "but I get to have two desserts." He smiled big, knowing it was Mitsy's week to be in charge of desserts.

"Okay, I will personally bring them to you," she said smiling. "I will see you then," she said turning to leave with the Pastor. She stopped and ran back to him and kissed David on his cheek. "Thank you," she said with a sweet smile. Mitsy quickly turned around and walked with the Pastor down the hallway.

David stayed on his knees on the floor for a few minutes. He was tired, confused, but at the same time he felt a deep sense of inner strength. He wondered if Mitsy was a special child. Could she be one of those that you read about in the magazines? He smiled to himself. In his self-absorbed habit, he was trying to make Mitsy out to be something special so he could be more special by helping her. He laughed at himself and realized that she was just a lonely child that needed help. Help that he could give to her. That was enough for anyone to handle.

He sat in the chair by the receptionist desk and placed his face in his hands. He knew in his heart that the Pastor was right. Somehow, someway, he and this fatherless child were spiritually connected. He decided right then not to question everything that was going on. He knew he must try to let it unfold as it should. He had spent his life trying to make things happen. In his sports, in his business, in his family, he was always the one trying to force the answers. He had no answer to the happenings of the last week. The events, some appearing to be imagined or delusions were too many and too powerful to fully grasp. He would have to see what happened next.

"As with any angel," he said out loud to himself. "Why does this child think that I am her angel?"

"Does it matter?" the young man said from behind the chair, startling David. "Does it really matter why she thinks that? The fact is," the young man said walking in front of David, "for today, she believes that is what you are. Is that such a bad thing?"

"And just who are you?" David said smiling at the young man. David wasn't sure if this young man was real, or a possible figment of his imagination.

"And who do you think that I am," the man said, mocking an intellectual tone.

"Are you the ghost of Richard Dunning?" David asked looking at the man's clothes.

"No way!" the man said confused, trying to determine what David was looking at. "Oh, I see. The clothes! No, poor Mr. Dunning is gone. And I mean long gone. I just like the clothes he had on the other night and decided to mimic them. I think they look good on me," the man said posing, "probably a new look that I will keep for a while. What do you think?"

"What I am thinking right now is crazy," David said.

"Which is?" the young man asked, straightening his tie.

"Am I right to guess that you are..." David paused, questioning his own sanity. There was a silence between them. David swallowed big and said, "Could I say that maybe, based on your obvious knowledge of last week and your appearance here today, that you are actually Mitsy's real guardian angel?"

"First," the man said toying with David, "that statement presumes that I am real. I don't think that anyone else has seen me. The Pastor? Mitsy? I believe you said something like, 'did you see that young whippersnapper that was just in here?'" The young man paused and shook his head. "I am perplexed at just what a whippersnapper actually is. I guess that is what I am. That is, of course, if you believe that I am real."

"Hmm…How did you put it, 'does it really matter?' I believe was your question," David said with a chuckle. "The fact is," David continued, "for today, I believe that you are real. I believe that you are probably Mitsy's angel. But you are letting her believe that I am her angel. Is that such a bad thing? For me to believe that about you? For her to believe that about me? It can only help her to believe…"

"You know, David," the man said with a sly grin, "you aren't as dumb as you look."

"Well, I resemble that remark!" David said with a hearty laugh. "It is my guess that one of two things will happen. You will disappear as I regain my senses and pull myself back together. Or possibly, God forbid, you are about to be my new buddy? Stalking me to make sure that I do your job of watching over Mitsy the way you think it should be done?"

"Oh, I think you're already figuring out the answer to that," the young man said.

"Yeah, I think I am," David said with a smile. "Since we will be spending a lot of time together, do you have a name?"

"Yeah, but you couldn't pronounce it," the man said sincerely. "We'll just have to make do and come up with a name sometime. Anyway, it's going to take a little while for you to deal with all of this." The young man looked at his watch and turned to walk away, "Well, places to go, people to see, things to do, lives to change. All of that angel sort of thing to do." He smiled over his shoulder at David. "Gotta go. It's been nice."

Then the young man disappeared thru the doorway into the hall.

David leaned back in the chair and closed his eyes. Fatigue weighted down his entire being.

CHAPTER 5

David sat still for the next few minutes and enjoyed the silence of the church office. He wasn't sure what was happening to him. Reality had turned surreal. The surreal was becoming real. He took a deep breath and opened eyes. No young man. No Mitsy. No Pastor. Just him in that chair, alone and quiet.

David thought for a moment that he should leave the church and drive straight to a hospital and check in. Though it was a good idea, David laughed to himself as he decided that he was too tired to deal with doctors' right then. The thought of trying to explain any of this in a way that seemed sane was even more tiring. He realized that, just as the paramedic Sissy had said last week about Mitsy, what he needed right then could not to be found in a pill or a needle. He closed his eyes again and leaned back in the chair.

Pastor Reynolds came bouncing back into the office as though he had just won a sweepstakes. "God is so good!" the Pastor said with great excitement, "so good!"

"And what has you walking two feet off of the ground?" David said leaning up in the chair.

"Well, David, you haven't been involved with that

child's life like I have," Pastor said seriously. "When her father was killed, she retreated into herself. She became very afraid. She has not felt really safe or secure since then. A really tragic situation. I have worked with her, the school psychologist has worked with her, her grandmother, Mrs. Lake, has been heaven sent. But Mitsy still walks around in a cloud of constant fear. We were afraid that we would eventually lose her."

"Jesus, Tom," David said sadly, "I didn't know that. You could never tell it to look at her."

"Oh, yes you could," Tom said, "or should I say, yes I could. And that everybody else could. But you never saw it, David, because she was different around you. She was always confident when she was close to you. So of course, you never could see the fear and insecurity that everyone else did. It wasn't present when you were around."

David remained silent. Pastor expected David to respond as he usually did, but David sat very quiet. He made no effort to challenge what the Pastor had just said.

"And when this incident happened last week," Tom cautiously continued, "we were afraid that it was going to put her over some edge that she would not be able to return from. You see, she has had this thing about angels since her father died. When she told her grandmother this morning the story that the paramedic had told her about the man's angel...well," Tom said, catching himself in his own enthusiasm, noticing the fatigue that loomed over David's being. "Well, anyway all of that is boring and can wait to another time," he said with a smile, "the fact of the matter is that she is finally feeling safe again. Thank you, Lord Jesus!"

"Well, good job, Tom," David said with sincere admiration, "you are a very loving and compassionate Pastor. I am glad that you were able to get thru to her..."

"No, David," Tom said jubilantly, "did you not hear her! Did you not hear her words? She says feels safe with you. You are the only person that has made her feel safe since her father's death. She told her grandmother as they were getting into the car that she knew that you were sent to watch over her. She said again that she felt as safe with you as she does with any angel. We are hoping that as long as you are around, maybe the other angels she talks about won't be an issue for her anymore. You can be her angel. A real one…"

"Maybe it's not me that she is talking about," David said very intensely, looking around the room to see if the young man was going to make a sudden appearance.

"What does that mean?" Tom asked amused, looking around trying to determine what David was looking for.

"You didn't happen to see a smart aleck young man in an expensive suit and Italian shoes leaving the building as you were coming back in did you, Tom?" David said with a slight chuckle.

"No," Tom said shrugging his shoulders, "I'm still yet to run into him. But if I do, I will certainly tell him you are looking for him."

"Ah, don't bother," David said standing and shaking Tom's hand. "I'm sure I'll run into him again. I've got to rest for a while. I'll see you tonight." David walked to the door.

"David," Tom said, "when things calm down, if you and I need to spend some time together, don't hesitate to let me know."

"Well, Pastor," David said smiling, "it may be too early to tell, but I think that you have killed two birds with one stone today. Maybe, as you said, helping Mitsy is what will help me get back to where I need to be in my own life. But if I feel an urge to, I'll definitely call you."

The two shook hands again and then hugged. Nothing more needed to be said.

David walked down the hallway pondering the strange turn of events that had completely disheveled his life in the past seven days. As he was unlocking his car he heard footsteps behind him. He turned thinking that Tom had come out behind him, but instead, he saw the young man walking past the trunk of his car.

"As with any angel? Who is that about?" David asked the young man, not really expecting an answer.

"Yeah, well, time will tell. Anyway, it's all working out isn't it," the young man said over his shoulder. "I mean, you aren't afraid any longer either are you, Mr. Hero?"

David looked down at the ground, paused a moment, and then said, "As a matter of a fact, I am not!" When he looked up, the young man was not to be seen.

David looked around the parking lot but it was empty. As he got into his car he knew it would be a while before he would be able to sort out the events of the past week. He was way too tired to deal with this young man, whoever or whatever he was. He would have to think about that later.

An intense feeling came over David as he started his car. He realized that fear can often be too strong for one person to bear alone. Perhaps, it can even become strong enough that human strength cannot overcome it. Everyone, sooner or later, will need help. From each other. And from God.

David knew that God had helped him. Then, in turn, he was able to help Mitsy. The paradox was that at the same time, they both had helped each other. David knew that regardless of how it had come about, of what things in the past several days were real or what may have been imagined, the crisis that had come into their lives had happened for a reason. It had brought with it a new sense of purpose for him. He knew the end result is what was most important, not the strange sequence of events. He and Mitsy both felt safe now. As safe as they would with any angel.

Made in the USA
Columbia, SC
13 March 2022